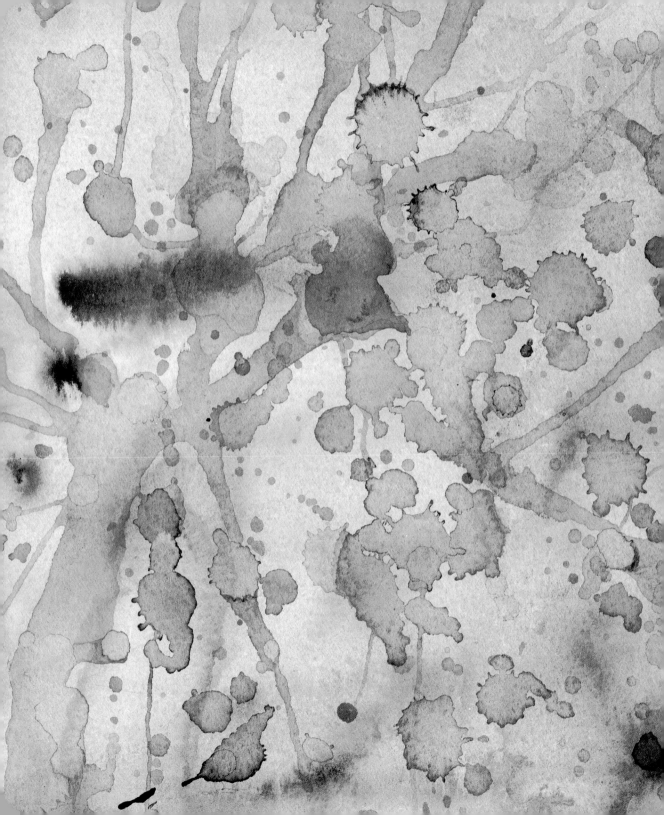

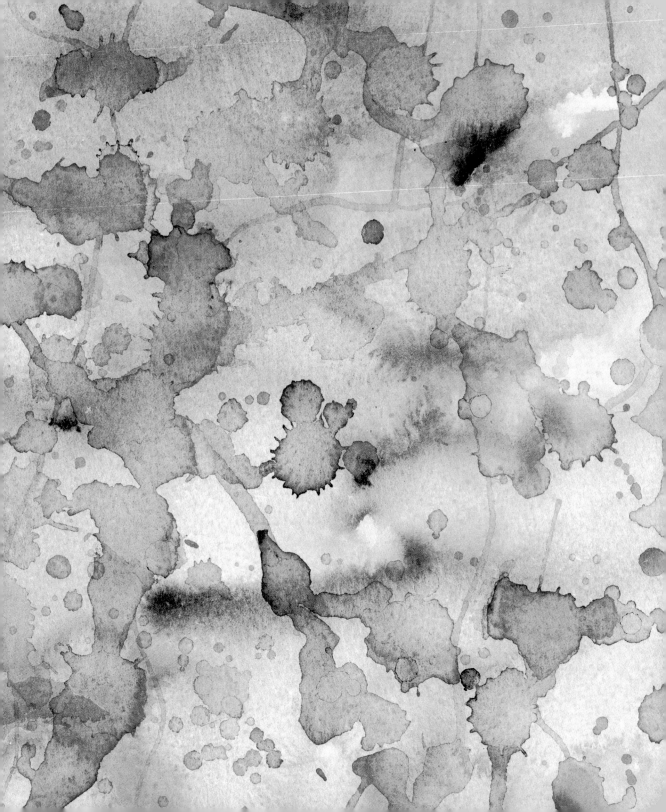

For Sue

First published 1994 by Walker Books Ltd
87 Vauxhall Walk, London SE11 5HJ

This edition published 2007

2 4 6 8 10 9 7 5 3 1

© 1994 Nick Sharratt

The moral right of the author has been asserted.

This book has been typeset in AT Arta.

Printed in China

British Library Cataloguing in Publication Data:
a catalogue record for this book is
available from the British Library.

ISBN 978-1-4063-0992-8

www.walkerbooks.co.uk

Caveman Dave

Nick Sharratt

WALKER BOOKS
AND SUBSIDIARIES

LONDON · BOSTON · SYDNEY · AUCKLAND

Caveman Dave
lives in a cave.

He doesn't
wash and
doesn't shave.

He's smelly but
he's very brave.

Wild animals don't
frighten Dave.

At bears and tigers
he will wave.

He tells fierce mammoths
to behave.

Dave really is
extremely brave —

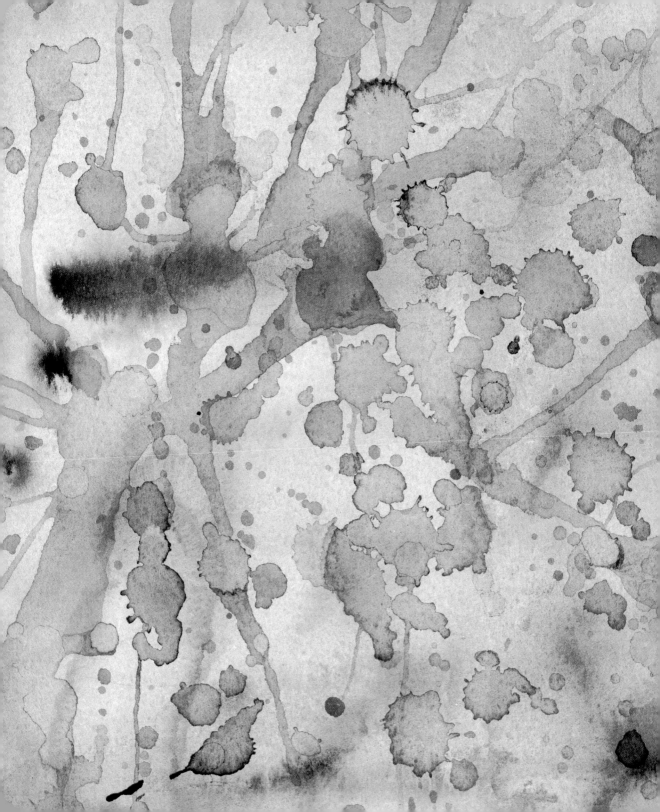

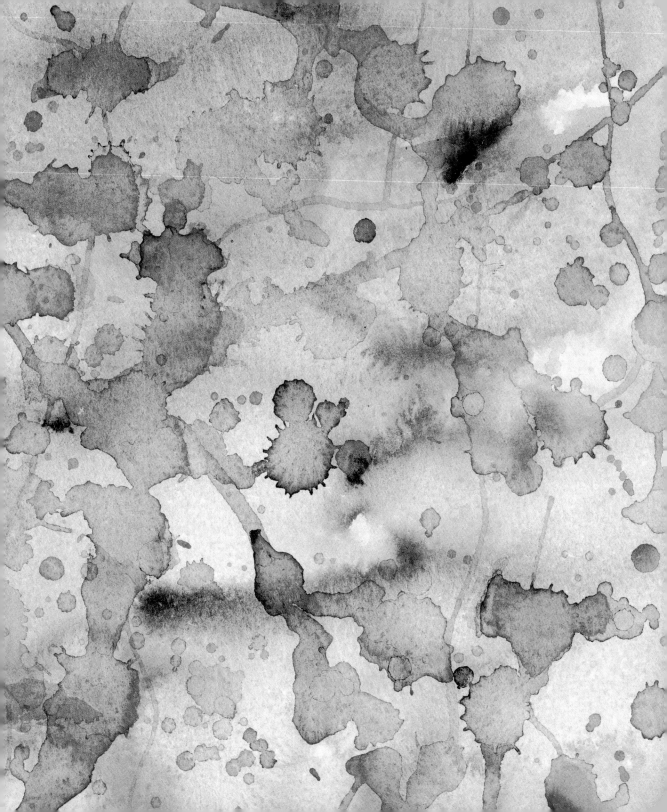